Written by David L. Burrier

Illustrated by Olena Vecchia Pittura

Smiling is a choice you make,
Even better when you laugh a lot!

To God be the Glory!

-David Burrier

Sir Lafůlot - Copyright © 2022
Author: David L. Burrier
Co-Author: Sherry A. Burrier

All Rights Reserved. No portion of this publication may be transmitted, reproduced, or stored in a retrieval system by any means including but not limited to, electronic, photocopy, recording, or any other form, without express written permission of the publisher. For information regarding permission please contact David Burrier and Craig Biss.

Edited and Published in Des Moines, IA. by Craig Biss. Imprint: Ballerina and the Bear Publishing.

Illustrations by Olena Vecchia Pittura © 2022

ISBN: 978-1-949439-10-6

Burrier Books titles may be purchased in bulk for educational, business, sales, promotional use, and fund-raising. For more information, please vist www.burrierbooks.com

Printed in the United States of America

Presented to:

_____

From:

_____

Date:

_____

A long time ago...

There was a village split down the middle;
Both sides lived in opposite ways.

One side Cheery, the other side Dreary;
They kept to themselves most days.

The Cheery side had a great leader whose name was Sir Lafŭlot.

Something about him was contagious that many around him had caught.

Sir Lafŭlot was a cheerful man
who always wore a smile.

No matter if something went wrong in his life,
he still spread happiness all the while.

Grumpy folks often changed their face
when they saw him come their way.

There was something about Sir Lafŭlot
that would always make their day.

Then one day a man named Cranky
tried to wipe the smile off his face.

By saying mean things to Sir Lafŭlot,
hoping his smile would erase.

But Sir Lafŭlot's smile would always remain
no matter how hard Cranky tried.

He even invited his friend Crabby
who left unsatisfied.

Then two more joined in to remove his smile;
their names were Moody and Snappy.

But no matter what they said or did,
Sir Lafŭlot still stayed happy.

Three more showed up who made every effort
to try to get him to stop;

But no matter how hard they shouted at him,
Smiles remained with Sir Lafŭlot.

One day there was a group playing
where all had smiles on their faces.

Though differently-abled, they chose to have fun,
even the child who walked with braces.

Gleeful and Giggles were part of this group.
They could play with one leg and one arm.

Other kids chose to include them;
to do so would cause no harm.

Morning till night Cheery children lived happy;
wherever you looked smiles remained.

Though each had their chores, mostly outdoors,
You seldom heard them complain.

The small boy in the wagon
even showed up for a ride.

His name is Jake from Dreary,
But he's being drawn to the Cheery side.

Jolly and Smiley lived with broken families
where they used to live with frowns.

Then one day they visited Sir Lafŭlot's group
where smiles turned to laughing sounds.

They learned that a frown is an upside-down smile
and how easy it is to reverse.

It's a choice you see; it was meant to be,
but for some it takes time to rehearse.

The Cheery group grew larger in numbers,
while the Dreary group steadily declined.

They learned life was no fun and troublesome
living in a negative frame of mind.

See, we all can be happy or we can be sad.
You have the power to choose.

Living Dreary or Cheery is all up to you,
it boils down to what you refuse.

Over time with lots of practice
they learned how to live more with smiles.

It just seemed more peaceful to live that way,
So they crossed over and changed their lifestyles.

Then one day the Villagers discovered
the Dreary side no longer existed.

The Cheery side became the way to live
where smiles and laughter persisted.

A very good lesson in life had been learned:
one common language is a smile.

Those who were Dreary for so many years
were sorry it took them a while.

They learned that with every change in seasons
there were bound to be ups and downs.

But living life with a smile on your face
felt better than living with frowns.

All this happened when years ago
a great leader lived a life that taught...

Smiling is a choice you make,
Even better when you laugh a lot!

Thank you Sir Lafŭlot.

1. Have you ever noticed when you show a huge smile on your face that others put a smile on theirs?

2. Did you know that a frown is an upside-down smile?

3. What happens when you put a smile on your face?

4. How does it change your mood?

5. How does it change the mood of those around you?

6. Would you rather wear a smile all day or a frown?

7. Do you know that it is easier to smile than to frown?

8. Do you know it takes more facial muscles to frown than it does to smile?

9. Are you drawn to someone who is smiling or frowning?

10. How does it make you feel when someone smiles at you?

11. Would you rather hang around someone who smiles and laughs a lot or someone who is 12. grumpy most of the time?

12. Would you rather live in a village where everyone is moody and dreary or one where people are happy and cheery?

It's your choice!

About the Author

David Burrier is a follower of Jesus, servent of God, children's author, award winning poet, motivational speaker, singer, songwriter, producer, master storyteller, and hope coach.

His mission in life is to be a source of inspiration, so that whoever he encounters will walk away with a renewed sense of mission and purpose in life.

David's life philosophy is guided by the following philosophical quote: "If you assume that every person you meet is hurting in some way, or fighting a battle you know nothing about, you will be right 99% of the time. So just be kind and seek to lift their spirit.

David is the founder of "I've Been There Ministries (IBTM), whose mission is "To bring the message of hope to a hurting world."

See David's live reading of his books on Youtube - Search Burrier Books.

You can read David's messages of hope at the IBTM Facebook page at facebook.com/ivebeenthereministries.

You can also find more inspiring information, resources, and how to schedule David to speak at ivebeenthereministries.com

Send all Facebook friend requests to David at www.facebook.com/davidburrier.56

You can email David directly at imfulofhope@hotmail.com

For more information about David's books please visit the Burrie' Children's book series at www.burrierbooks.com

About the Illustrator

Olena Vecchia Pittura is a popular children's book illustrator who lives in Sofia, Bulgaria. She studied at the National Art Academy of Bulgaria. She is recognized as one of the best illustrators in the business and is highly sought after by authors throughout the world.

To contact Olena Vecchia Pittura please follow her on social media.

About the Publisher

Craig Biss is an American children's book author, consultant, editor, and owner of the Ballerina and the Bear Publishing, located in San Antonio, TX. He is the proud father of three amazing children. Craig is a strong supporter of homeschooling and Christian-based curriculum. He is a veteran of the military and graduated with his master's degree in Homeland Security with a focus on counter-terrorism.

Craig has written and self-published three children's books and is working on his first novel. To purchase any of Craig's works, please visit www.amazon.com

For more information about Craig please contact craig.biss@ballerinabearpublishing.com

Read the entire Burrie' Childrens Books collection...

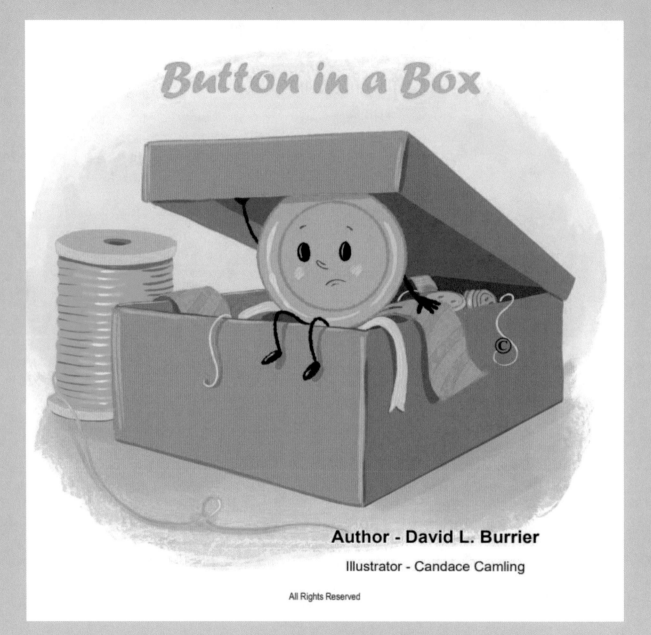

Button in a Box

Author - David L. Burrier

Illustrator - Candace Camling

All Rights Reserved

www.burrierbooks.com

Read the entire Burrie' Childrens Books collection...

The Ballerina and The Bear

The STRING THING!

Author - David L. Burrier

Illustrator - Anne Celesta Stevens

All Rights Reserved

www.burrierbooks.com

Read the entire Burrie' Childrens Books collection...

www.burrierbooks.com

Read the entire Burrie' Childrens Books collection...

www.burrierbooks.com

Sir Lafŭlot
by author
David L. Burrier

"The ones who are crazy enough to think they can change the world, are the ones who do."

This story demonstrates how one man changed the world around him with a simple smile and how dreary became cheery over time.

The IYQ symbol is significant to the Sir Lafŭlot story. When people read out loud the letters left to right, you have the opportunity to respond by saying, "Thanks! IYQ 2!" You're instantly able to make them happy and I guarantee (at a minimum) it will put a smile on their face. It might seem silly or childish, but my use of those three letters on the IYQ button or on my hat or shirt have put a smile on the faces of thousands of people over the years, lifting their spirit and putting joy in their life. This story shows the power of a simple smile and encourages you to be so happy that when others look at you, they become happy too!

You're going to have fun reading this book because our illustrator has hidden the IYQ symbol on every page. Your challenge is to see if you can find it buried in every illustration including the cover. You can make a game out of who can find it first.

Have fun reading and don't forget the discussion guide at the back of the book to learn more how you too can change the world around you with a simple smile!

And always remember...
I Y Q 2!

Made in the USA
Monee, IL
04 March 2023

28331955R00026